THE THREE NAUGHTY SISTERS MEET
Bluebeard

by R. Capdevila

illustrated by M. Company

English version by Marilyn Malin

METHUEN CHILDREN'S BOOKS . LONDON

One day the Three Naughty Sisters had been *specially* naughty – they had splashed soap suds all over the floor of the passage, so that everyone went slipping and sliding (the little mice loved that). They were made to mop it up; but then they had to stand with their faces to the wall, out of harm's way. Suddenly the Wicked Witch appeared.

'Ho ho!' said the Witch, cackling. 'Just look at these naughty little girls.'

'Oh, go away, you silly old witch,' said Sally rudely. 'You're not much of a witch anyway – and your spells never work.'

'We'll see about that!' said the Witch angrily. She took a handful of herbs from her basket and began to chant:

> Three little girls all alike,
> Naughty triplets full of tricks;
> Just see me take a hand
> and send you into story book land.

'And you won't come back!' she added gleefully.

The Three Naughty Sisters giggled – but they soon stopped laughing when they found themselves being carried off . . . far, far away.

'Look,' cried Molly. 'There's a castle! I wonder who lives there. Let's ask.' 'Good day,' said Sally very politely to some people who were coming along the road. 'Could you tell us, please, whose castle that is?'

'Don't you know?' said the man surprised. 'That's Bluebeard's castle.' And he shuddered as he said it. 'He's the one who locked up his wives in damp dark dungeons. He's wicked and cruel!'

Jilly and Molly clung together, but Sally wasn't frightened.

'I'm going to explore,' she said.

She led the way to the open door
of the towering castle.

'What a magnificent castle!' they exclaimed when they were inside. 'It's enormous.' They hid behind a curtain as they heard footsteps coming.

In came a tall, heavy man with a thick blue beard which covered half his face. He was pulling behind him a young woman who looked very scared. When they stopped near the door, he said to her: 'Here are the keys of the castle. You can enter all the rooms, except the cellar. That is forbidden, on pain of death! And now, kiss me!'

The poor young woman was sitting weeping when Sally, Jilly and Molly came out from behind the curtain. 'Hello,' said Sally, 'we'd love to see the castle, may we look round?' (This was a good moment for one of the little mice to have a rest.)

'Look round!' said the young woman in amazement, never before had she seen three girls so alike. 'Don't you know what Bluebeard is like? He hates children and if he catches you, he'll make mincemeat out of you!'

'But he's not here,' said Jilly. 'Please, do let us look round.' They begged so hard that the young woman finally gave in. 'Very well,' she said, 'but then you must leave immediately,' and she led the way to the kitchens. The sisters enjoyed that very much and so did the mice.

Next they went to the Great Hall, and hid in the suits of armour. Then the young woman, who was Bluebeard's wife, said: 'Now you *must* go'. 'Oh no!' cried the Three Naughty Sisters. 'We haven't seen the cellar yet!'

And again they begged and pleaded so hard that the young woman gave in. She, too, was curious to know what lay behind the forbidden door.

When they got to the door, the young woman tried
to open it. She tried key after key till finally, with
the last key but one, the lock turned.

They pushed the door open – and there was Bluebeard, brewing a magic potion in an enormous pot!

'Oh-oh-oh!' cried the young woman in terror.

'Ahhh!' growled Bluebeard. 'You've disobeyed me, you wicked wife.

Now you'll learn what happens to those who discover my secret!'

Things really began to happen. The Three Naughty
Sisters were so frightened that they forgot they were
in a fairy story and weren't supposed to interfere.
They decided to trick Bluebeard and save his wife.
'Run, run!' Molly shouted.

Just in time they spied a little door in the corner and
they all rushed through. But behind the door, a
huge ditch, deep and evil smelling was full of –
crocodiles! What could they possibly do? 'There's no
time to lose. I'm going to jump,' Sally cried.

The other girls followed her into the water and so did the young woman. Bluebeard watched as seven fierce crocodiles swam towards them, snapping their jaws . . . and then –

'Ho ho ho!' they heard. It was the Wicked Witch cackling. 'Now you see what happens to naughty little girls. The crocodiles are going to eat you all up!'

'It's only a story. They're not real!' screamed Sally.
  'Not real! Just you wait and see!' laughed the witch.
  'Goodbye, goodbye my little dears.'
  Bluebeard sat chuckling on the side. He was
enjoying himself.

'If it's a story', thought Molly, 'then anything is possible.' She seized the eraser she had in her pocket and began to rub vigorously at the leading crocodile. In a second he had disappeared. Jilly grabbed her pencil and drew a rope leading up to the highest part of the wall and Sally began to climb. They were saved!

Bluebeard was very put out, and the Witch? She was absolutely furious.

'Why can I never win against those Three Naughty Sisters?' the Witch grumbled. But she had to agree they'd won and she packed them off home.

'If you're naughty again, there'll be a far, far worse adventure!' she threatened. The Three Naughty Sisters laughed. They looked forward to that!

Published in Great Britain in 1986
by Methuen Children's Books Ltd
11 New Fetter Lane, London EC4P 4EE
Published in Spain by Editorial Ariel SA
under the title *Las Tres Mellizas Y . . .*
Copyright © 1985 by R Capdevila and M Company
English version by Marilyn Malin copyright © 1986
by Methuen Children's Books Ltd

ISBN 0 416 61320 9

Printed in Spain